Alexander's Sock

Alexander's Sock

Isabel D. Prucha

VANTAGE PRESS
New York

Illustrated by Tanya Stewart

FIRST EDITION

Published by Vantage Press, Inc.
419 Park Ave. South, New York, NY 10016

Manufactured in the United States of America
ISBN: 0-533-14849-9

Library of Congress Catalog Card No.: 2004090511

0 9 8 7 6 5 4 3 2 1

Alexander's Sock

Episode 1: It Happened!

I always thought it was cool watching kids and grownups with casts on some part of their bodies. I liked it when I saw a kid with a fat white arm that showed scribbling all over. At school when someone showed up with a cast on some part of their body, they became an instant celebrity. All the kids, including myself, jumped at the opportunity to write something on their leg, arm, ankle, or whatever. Always, the boy or girl with the cast was smiling from ear to ear with all the attention they got. It was also cool to read the nonsense some of the kid's friends wrote down. Some of the writing was downright stupid, like;

"Hope you break the other leg."

"I hope you get an itch."

"I wish I were you."

"Some people do anything for attention."

"What do you do when you go to the toilet?"

"You're cool."

"Get real!"

All this scribbling is really funny when you're the one writing it and you hope it makes someone laugh. It's a whole new story when you're the one wearing the cast. Boy, have I learned some good lessons. I had to wear one of those suckers for what seemed an eternity. I know my Dad said my cast weighed less than five pounds but it felt like fifty to me.

My misfortune came when I least expected it. It was actually a night out for my family, my mom, dad, and sister, Nicole. We'd gone out to dinner at our favorite Chinese restaurant before attending a school function. We had enjoyed the sweet-and-sour pork, the chow mein, and all that nice warm tea. But our favorite was reading our fortune cookie statements out loud. I don't even remember what it said now. It was something like, "You are in for a wonderful surprise." Believe me, it was anything but wonderful!!

After we all shared our good fortunes, we left for a school function. It was something like "back-to-school" night and my sister, Nicole, and I were getting a little bored just following the adults around the school. We were in the cafeteria scouting out the refreshments when I wandered over near to where my dad was standing. I leaned my body against a huge table that was tipped against the wall. I recall barely touching it and the whole structure started toward me. As the end of the table pushed me, it tipped my upper body forward and I felt myself falling. I was definitely in a state of panic as I started for the floor. In a split second my dad responded almost subconsciously.

He caught my fall and the movement of the table from the corner of his eye and threw his arm forward to catch the table. My dad's pretty strong. He managed to hold most of the weight of the table and keep it from slamming on top of me. But my right leg was not so lucky. It got pinned under a corner of the monster table. Wow, I saw stars, and without shame, I began to scream in pain. My dad lifted the collapsed table completely off my right foot and tried to calm me down. His expression told me that I had really done something major to my leg.

My parents are almost telepathic because my mother appeared from nowhere having recognized my scream—I guess. Anyway, Nicole, my sister, came running toward me with teary eyes in sympathy for my pain. By this time my dad had lifted me and said something to my mom who quickly grabbed Nicole and made for the door. Everyone in the cafeteria was concerned and wanted to call 911 but my dad said, "I can drive him to the hospital faster." No one contradicted him and so he took me to our car and by this time my foot felt like it was on fire and weighed a ton. At the same time the pain felt like electrical shocks going through my foot up my leg. Needless to say, I was not a quiet passenger en route to the hospital. My poor family was most understanding though. My dad stayed real cool just saying, "Everything is going to be alright, Alexander." He would also add, "We're almost there, really."

Thinking back, maybe a trip in an ambulance would have been enough to calm me down listening to the siren, or at least it would have drowned my screams. But, I'll never know. We got to the hospital in a flash, according to my sister. To me it seemed like forever. Despite my pain and screams, I was conscious of the big hospital doors that automatically swallowed us into the hospital and into the emergency unit. A nurse came and asked if we needed a wheelchair but my dad said no. She then proceeded to reassure me that everything was going to be okay. I didn't feel reassured at all since the pain did not go away.

While Mom dealt with the paperwork, Dad took me into a big bright room where I was stretched onto a very narrow bed/table. It seemed hours before a man in a green outfit came in and was all smiles. He wasn't going to get a smile from me in my condition. He conferred with my dad after taking a look at my foot. I was still making quite a loud commotion so I did not hear what they said. Soon I found out that the doctor decided that I had had enough pain for one night. They gave me some medicine that put me somewhat out of my misery almost in seconds. It felt like when you go to the dentist to have a tooth filled and they prick you with a needle and then your gums, tongue and cheek feel humongous. I kept looking at my ankle to make sure it wasn't getting as big as I felt it was.

About now I think my mom peeked through the door to see how I was doing. She looked in just in time to see a nurse start to cut my fairly new blue jeans. The expression on her face told me that she was not too happy. I could see her mind working as she saw two-thirds of the pant leg drop to the floor. She saw my worried look and came over to me and said, "Don't worry, I got them on a good sale and I'm sure I can find you another pair." There was no time for me to worry. Now that I was calmer, it was time to take a good look at the damage with x-rays. This is where I began to take in what was happening to me. Two nurses took the brakes off the bed in which I lay and began to roll it out the wide door and down the hall. My dad was not about to be left behind. He followed right along by my side to the end of a long hallway where two wide doors opened. The sign above the doors said, "X-ray." I stayed on the narrow bed while the young lady in the x-ray room gently moved my ankle into different positions and after each repositioning, she would say, "Hold real still." Then she would go behind a little glass door and I could hear the click of the camera above my ankle. She was gentle and soft-spoken. I was tempted to tell her that it didn't hurt very much anymore but decided not to. I didn't want anybody getting careless with my leg and then I would have the pain back. She turned my foot left and right and upright for the photos. Then I was wheeled back to the emergency room. My dad stayed with me the whole time except when the actual pictures were being taken. Something about radiation and how people should not be exposed to it. But Dad kept saying that everything was going to be alright. Somehow I knew otherwise. My brain began to work and I wondered how I was going to manage my daily activities. All of a sudden, I knew that my soccer skills were going to suffer and I would probably not be as famous as I had planned. But, I didn't share this with my dad. He coaches my soccer team!

We were back in that room where the lights kept getting brighter and brighter and my eyes kept feeling like sand was in them. The waiting was getting to all of us. Nicole would peek into the room and just give me a faint smile. My mom would come in and give me a kiss on the cheek and rub my head lovingly. It was now well past midnight and the emergency room was busier. I'm sure there were more serious cases than my poor ankle but to me it felt like someone had gone and forgotten we were there waiting and waiting. Finally, the same man in green, the doctor, popped in with two x-rays in his hand. He showed my dad (as I looked on from the side) where the break had occurred. The doctor explained that I had been very lucky as the break was just about half an inch above the growth plate. He went on to say that the break was a clean one. A clean break to me meant that there would be no blood seeping out of my body anytime soon. I was grateful for that because my ankle was now turning a little purple and looking swollen.

The doctor proceeded to tell us that a cast was in order. When I heard this, my spirits actually were lifted. I could see myself the object of everyone's envy when I went to school the next day. For a little while I didn't even care that time was passing and my cast was not coming. Finally, they got their act together—that is, the nurses and the doctor. They came in with what looked like a pan of hot water and a thick wad of bandage. Then they proceeded to cut even more of my pant leg. It was then I realized that I was to have a cast almost long enough to reach my groin.

First they put a couple of splints on my leg, and then the team worked slowly, wrapping white wet gauze around the leg. It seemed they took forever to smooth out each little wrinkle as they dipped it in water, which produced a chalky goo that went round and round my leg. It looked like they were building a big tube of papier mâché. By the time they were finished wrapping my leg in an enormous cast, it was past one-thirty A.M. My leg was a little bent and all I could see were my toes sticking out at the bottom. They looked chalky as

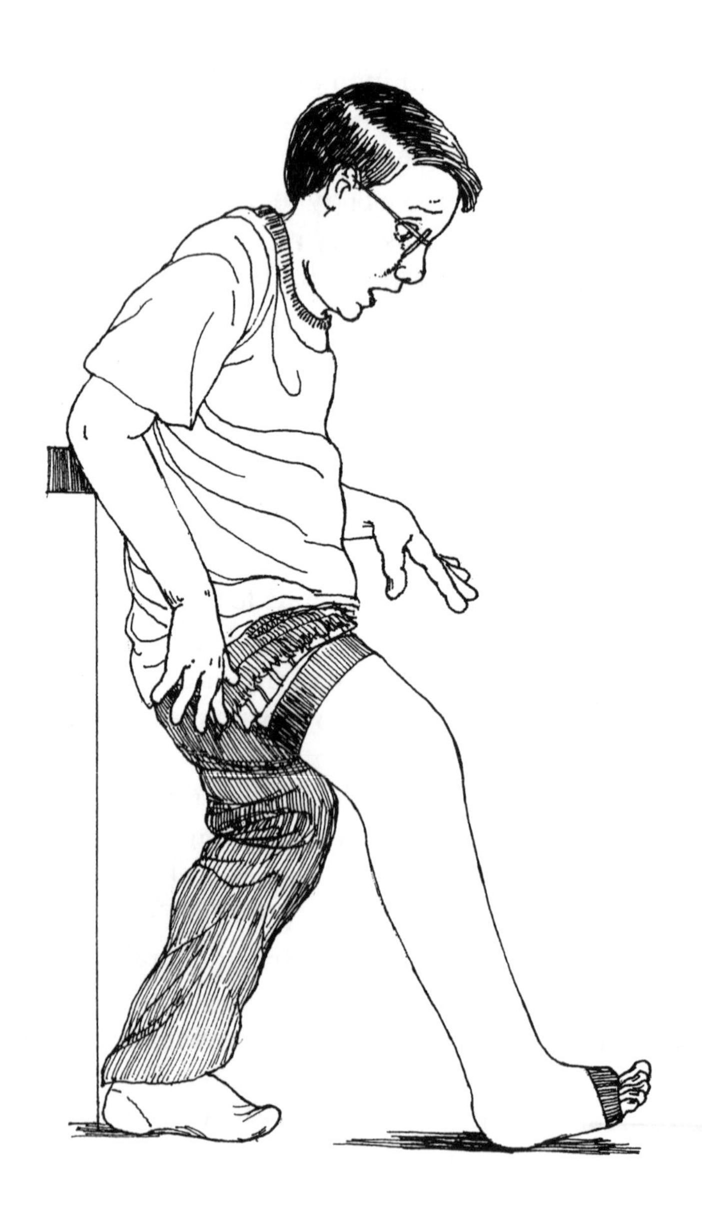

well. I just knew my mom would wash them off before I could get into my bed. She's very neat that way.

Still feeling woozy, the doctor announced that I could try standing up. Oh, my gosh, I was simply not prepared for the weight of that huge sock. Suddenly, I was petrified at the thought that I was going to have to lug that thing around for months. The pain I felt was not severe but the tears kept coming even though I tried not to cry. My dad came to the rescue again. He said, "Don't worry, you'll do fine and we're all here to help you." But all I could think was, *how will I ever get to the bathroom?*

A nurse appeared through the door with a wheelchair and my dad helped me hobble over to it. Then a little table was lifted from under the chair that allowed my leg to rest on it, elevated from the floor. I think both my dad and I were relieved that he would not have to carry me to the car, cast and all!! I'm not exactly skinny and the weight of the cast added at least fifty pounds—or so it seemed. We left the emergency room and my dad stood beside me as the nurse wheeled me toward my mom and Nicole. I was tired and sleepy but still under the influence of the pain medication. I could see that Nicole and Mom were also worn out. I felt badly that I had put them through this whole ordeal but then I saw Nicole's eyes pop out as she saw the size of the cast. And, of course, the first thing she said was, “Can I be the first to write something on it?” The nurse said she had to wait until it was completely dry—probably by morning. Nicole beamed when I said, “Sure, no problem.” My mom was more down to earth. She asked, “How does it feel?” I just said, “Heavy, very heavy.”

The trip home from the hospital was quieter than the trip to the hospital. I was actually afraid to share my real concerns over what lay ahead for me, so I kept quiet. Everyone else was too exhausted to make conversation.

Episode 2: Home at Last!

It was way past two A.M. when we got home and exhaustion was our middle name. I couldn't wait to get to the bathroom. Nature was calling. My dad carried me into the house and put me down on one of the kitchen chairs. I was also dying of thirst. We are big water drinkers in my family. But when I asked for some water or juice, both my mom and dad looked at each other as if I had asked for a candy bar at that hour of the morning. My mom simply told me that perhaps I should not take too much liquid into my body because I would have to go to the bathroom more frequently. Her comment only reminded me that I had to make a call right then and there. I grimaced and my dad asked what the matter was. I just told him that I had an urgent call to make—could he help me to the bathroom. In my slumped condition I needed all the help I could get.

I did not realize how much help I would need until my dad practically carried me into the bathroom at the end of the hall. Once in the bathroom we both looked at the toilet and then at my right leg, trying to assess the best approach to relieving myself. First I struggled with turning myself around so that my back would be to the toilet; next, my dad balanced me and told me to try sitting down. That did not work too well because the weight on my right side threw me off balance and I almost landed in the bathtub. My dad held on to me and finally said to try it the other way around after making sure that I had to go #1.

Still, pulling what was left of my pants down was a challenge because the cast was almost up to my groin. With much difficulty I managed to get the right part of my body facing in the right direction and aimed into the middle of the toilet. All of a sudden my body tensed up and I could not urinate. Only minutes before I was desperate, but now nothing was happening. My dad told me to relax, but I simply could not calm down. I was very worried. After a little while nature took its course and I felt better. Once the bathroom ordeal was over my dad helped me to my bedroom.

In my bedroom, I looked around from my sitting position on the bed, sort of looking for my pajamas. My mom walked in just then and read my thoughts.

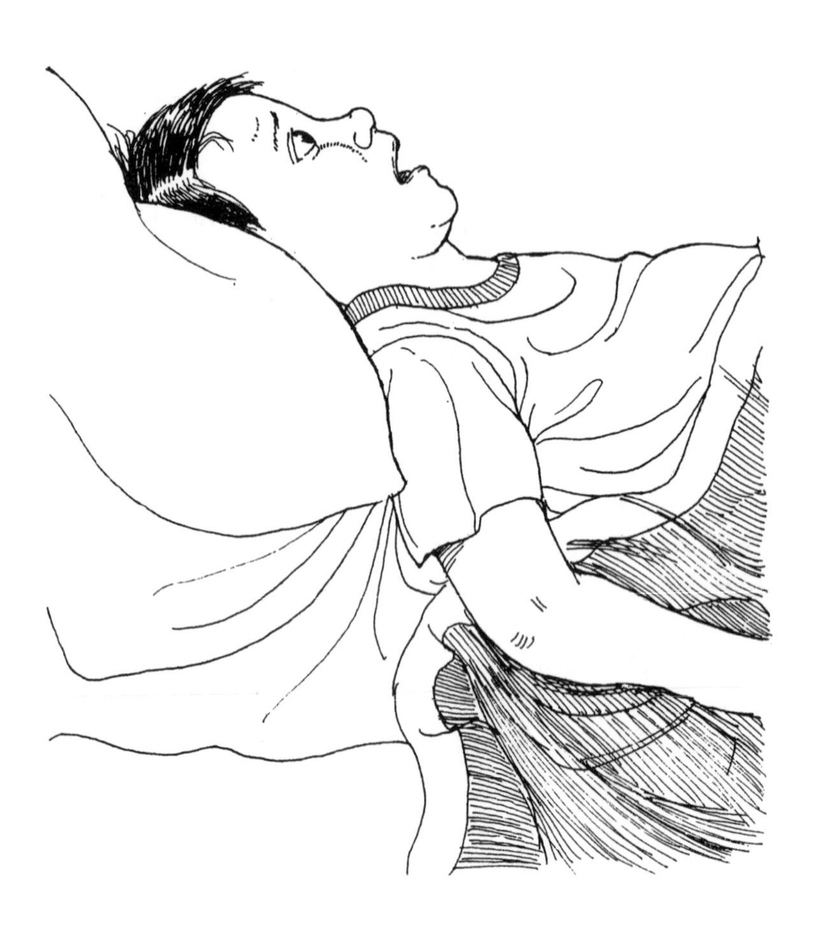

She just said not to worry about pajamas for tonight. She said she would figure something out for tomorrow. I guess she was wondering which pair of pajamas to tear up so that my right leg could fit into them. In the meantime my dad straightened me out on the bed so I could land on my pillow and I was only too willing because I was exhausted. My sister had conked out almost immediately after getting into the house. She just quietly went into her room and never came out again. We didn't even hear a weak "goodnight" from her.

That first night was not so bad because I was still on the pain pills they gave me in the hospital. One of them knocked me out pretty soon too. However, I was not as lucky as Nicole. Sleeping on my back is not my favorite position for sleeping. Every time I tried to turn onto my left side, it was next to impossible to move the iron sock. Since turning onto my stomach would require lifting the right leg over, that too was out of the question because of the weight. So, I did the next best thing in coping with my situation, I sought comfort from my parents who heard my moaning and crying and came in to try to make me more comfortable.

In time, we did manage to make things better in getting me ready for bed. My parents would help me to lie on my left side by putting my right leg over it and I managed to sleep several hours that way. From that position I was able to just slide myself onto my back and managed the second half of the night. As I gained more confidence and strength, I even managed to lift the sock on my own by picking it up with my hands and dropping it to one side.

Episode 3: The Challenge of School

Attending school was definitely not a piece of cake! Of course, the first day after the accident my parents agreed that perhaps it was best for me to stay home. I was still pretty much a wreck after taking the medication I got and the lack of sleep. My appetite diminished since I was preoccupied with how I was going to accomplish simple tasks like getting out of bed, getting dressed, going to the bathroom again, showering, getting to the kitchen for meals. . . . And the list of worries only kept increasing in my mind. My family was super but they all had things to do, so they could not attend to me every minute of the day. However, my parents put a lot of effort into getting me to use the crutches.

The crutches became like large chopsticks under my armpits. I kept trying to move them one at a time but I kept leaving my body behind so I had to learn to co-ordinate lifting myself with my weight on my left foot and then moving forward with both crutches hitting the floor at the same time. It was hard to believe how clumsy I was. Between the weight of my big sock and the soreness in my armpits, I thought I was in as much pain as when I was in the hospital. My parents assured me that things would get better, but I did not believe them.

However, my fame was just beginning. It so happened that the big SAT annual testing was scheduled for the day after my accident. Well, it never occurred to me that the test was such a big deal, but the principal of the school apparently thought otherwise. She showed up at our house in the early afternoon with all the paperwork for me to be tested. I couldn't believe that the principal made house calls. Not only did she come prepared to test me, she also came prepared to feed me one of my very favorite delicacies—sushi! So there I was plowing ahead with the test in order to hurry up and begin on the sushi. *Not a bad start for an invalid*—or so I thought. I was also dreaming of how I was going to use this special visit as a conversational piece in school when I went back.

Staying home the second day after I got my big sock was not an option. My parents woke me up with calm but firm voices which instantly told me that it was no use asking to stay home again. My dad adjusted the crutches so that they were a better fit and I managed to go to the bathroom on my own early in the morning. I even felt like a real magician getting out from under my crutches and balancing my weight on my good leg in order to clutch the wash basin with one hand. With the other hand, I worked on getting my clothes off. Going number one was not a problem. The problem came when I had to sit down. I was soon to find out that the perils that awaited me in school were even more frustrating. One thing I knew for sure, I could not wait until the last minute to excuse myself from my classroom to go to the toilets.

Even though I had a slight headache, probably from the medicines, I decided not to complain about it. My dad helped me get into the car by picking me up so that I went into the backseat with my big sock first and then the rest of my body slid into place. My dad instructed me that when I got out, someone would open the car door next to my toes and I was to slide my big sock out first and then push my behind forward and the rest would be a piece of cake. It sounded okay, but when we got to school I was so nervous that I felt like I had dug a hole in the back seat and I could not lift my butt off the seat in order to slide myself out feet first. We must have looked pretty funny because both my mom and Nicole were pulling me out the door and in the process pulled a bit too hard so that I banged my forehead on the car frame. It wasn't bad but it was not a good way to start my day in school.

However, once I was standing and under my crutches, I felt like a rock star because everyone was looking at me or pointing me out to some of the other kids. This gave me enough courage to put on a great show. I asked my mom to let go of me so that I could manage to get to my classroom. I ambled down the corridor—my classroom was not far from the parking lot, thank goodness. The minute I got to the door someone from behind me quickly came to my rescue and opened the door for me. Kind gestures are not always there in a middle school. Then the fun began.

Kids circled around me and wanted all the details. Some came running toward me with their pens and pencils. The teacher let me have my moment of glory before calling everyone to attention and back to their seats. She told everyone not to tire me too much and suggested they could write their good wishes on my sock at recess time. This seemed to satisfy everyone and before five minutes were up the whole class was back to the normal routine except for me. Being right handed meant that my right leg went under the writing table. Wrong. With the heavy sock it was difficult to manipulate my leg under the desk very well. Then there was the thing about the crutches—where to put them.

I could not just slide them under my desk for they would interfere with either the student in front or the student in back of me—if I put them on the aisle, someone could trip over them. Another option was for someone to lean them against the blackboard but then I could not get to them. Finally, the teacher came to my rescue and slid them under my desk and under the student in front of me with a warning to be careful when he stood up.

At recess the autographing continued and I was especially pleased with all the little dainty hearts that a lot of the girls drew on my cast. I was even inspired to think that this meant the beginning of a real eventful school year for me. However, my romantic fantasies were short lived. They became just fantasies in my mind as I later discovered that girls tend to draw hearts on everything they can get their hands on and the heart means nothing at all.

I don't remember being too productive that morning. I was very worried about having to exit to the toilet. My mom said she would check on me at recess since she worked in the front office. But who wants their mother taking them to the toilet in front of all their friends?? So I had asked her not to come see me, but by 9:30 A.M., I was beginning to regret it. At last recess came and I did not have to make a mad dash.

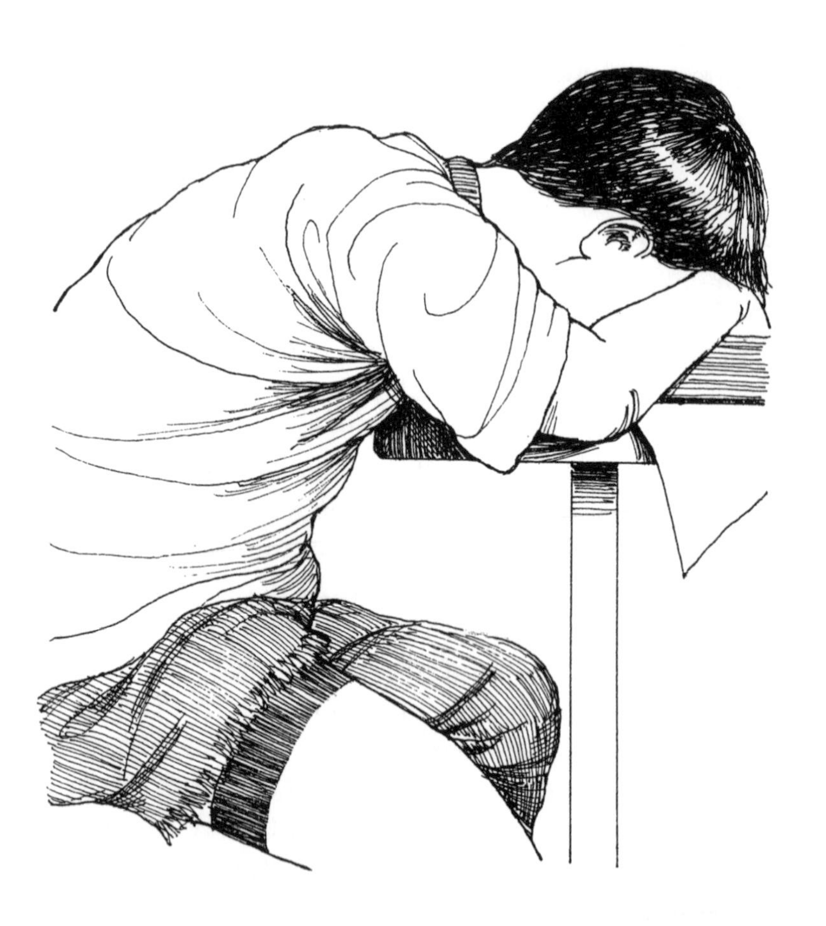

Instead, I was surrounded by my classmates eager to write their nonsense on my sock. I loved the attention and just sat on a bench while everyone took their turn. Not everyone got to write something so I told them to look for me at lunch time.

Before lunch time I definitely had a problem. Luckily my teacher had had experience with such difficulties, so she called the front office for Mom. Mom was wonderful. She came in and said it was time for me to take some medicine and she helped me out of the classroom. We made it to the bathroom before it was mobbed. The stalls are small so it was hard to maneuver myself around the space but eventually I even managed to close the door behind me. My mom kept asking from outside the door if I needed help but I was determined to manage on my own, and I did!

The afternoon went very slowly, and lugging that big cast around made me tired. I think I even fell asleep on my desk because the girl behind me gave my chair a slight push to stir me up. I think she thought I might've died there in front of her. By the time the dismissal bell rang, I was ready to go home. I got help with my crutches and I slowly made my way to the door where Nicole and Mom greeted me. Now the trick was how to get into the car. Dad was not around to pick me up and slide me in feet first.

So, I told my mom that I would turn myself around, sit on the seat and she could pull me from the other side. While huffing and puffing, it took Mom and Nicole a good five minutes to pull me in. Needless to say, when we got home and I got to my room, I collapsed on my bed and slept for four hours. When I woke up I had a good cry and told my parents I was not going back to school, it was too hard on me because the sock was too heavy. I should have known my parents were bright because they had already figured out a solution. They had decided that a wheelchair was what I needed. They had contacted the hospital and were told where to get one, what size, and what type to get. So when I came out of my bedroom and went to the kitchen for dinner, there was the wheelchair waiting for me.

The third day was again an adventure because now I had a wheelchair and that caused a bit of a commotion. The trick was finding a table of sorts for me to use as a desktop. Finally, I was just positioned next to a left-handed desk on the aisle and all I had to do was lean over on the desk table and do my work. The wheel chair even had a feature where I could extend my injured leg and keep it propped. So, I did not have to wear myself out with its weight.

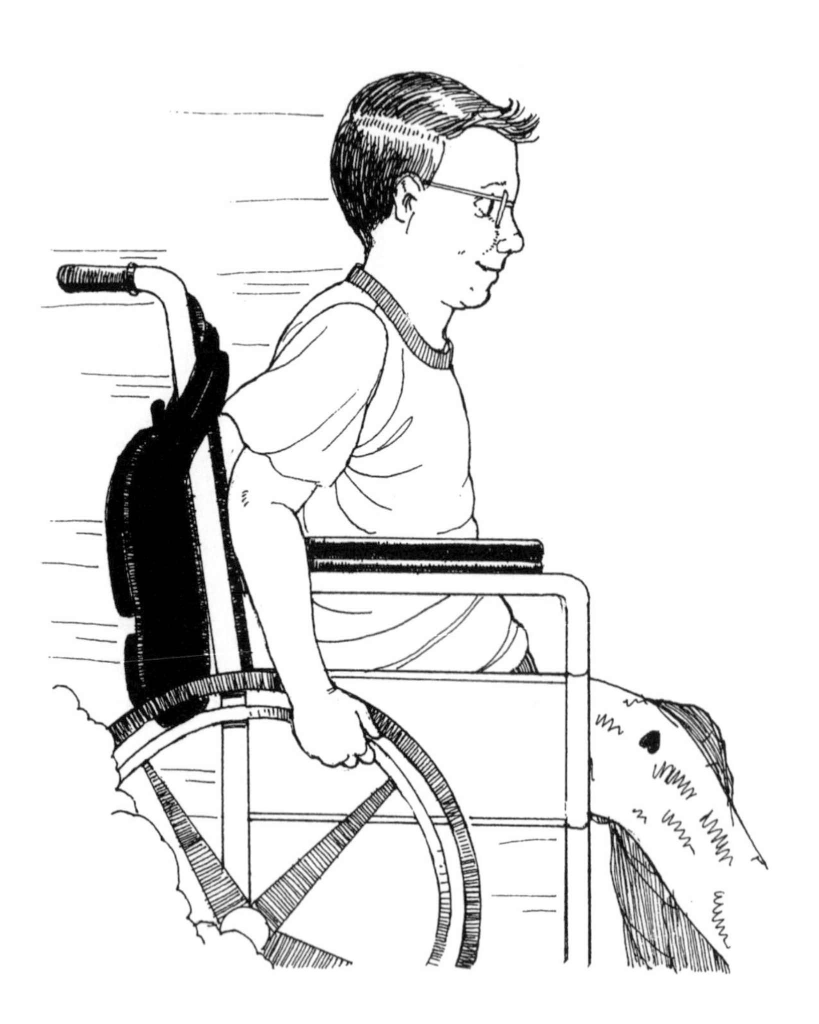

Eventually things became routine and as I learned to drive my wheel chair, I also became pretty good at switching from wheelchair to crutches and I could do a pretty good run down the corridors and into the library, toilet, cafeteria and make my way around the school. I learned to appreciate what handicapped people live with on a daily and permanent basis. It is so easy to take little things for granted, like stooping down to pick up a pencil. In a wheelchair or on crutches your balance can be lost in a blink, and off your body goes tumbling down. My whole family learned how difficult it is for families with a handicapped person to eat out in restaurants. There are some that have no facilities such as wide doors, or wide aisles to move with a wheelchair. I prayed every night that I would be alright at the end of six weeks when my sock was to come off. I did not want to be tied to the wheelchair or the crutches for life. I was blessed that my injury was not permanent, but it seemed that I had to be reminded of it daily by my parents.

Episode 4: My Wardrobe

As a rule, kids really pay attention to what they wear to school. I guess everyone wants to make a good impression and be noticed—and basically, I'm no different. The name of the game in schools is being popular and you do not become popular unless you are noticed. I can't say that I was either very popular or much noticed in my school but after my accident my fears of becoming a total unknown became real. You see, my wardrobe was instantly reduced to boxer shorts instead of briefs and jeans that had been cut off.

The cutoff jeans were not a bad deal by themselves. What was bad was that one leg had to be longer than the other and hiding the seam of my boxer shorts was a nuisance. I had to deal with that problem every time I got up from a chair. I had to pull the wrinkled edge of my cast leg shorts that got caught in the groin and smooth it down in order for the boxer shorts not to show. My left side was not a problem, of course. On top of it all, the jean leg that was cut off also had to be slit up the side seam in order to provide enough width for the cast to go over it. So I was paranoid about exposing a little peek at my underwear. But, what can I say, kids are funny that way. That is the sort of thing that kids use to poke fun and ridicule someone in schools. No doubt about it, my age group can be cruel. So I was out there trying to protect myself from any possible humiliation.

While I was busy worrying about nonsense, my mother was being practical in getting a workable wardrobe for me. We were lucky that my accident occurred in the late summer and early autumn when the weather in California is wonderful—sunny, not too hot and not cold at all. Although I don't normally have an excessive amount of clothes in my wardrobe, I do think I have enough variety to change pants and tee-shirts during the week so as not to look too dull every day. But, all that changed when my need for a baggy and wide right pant leg became a priority. Obviously, I did not expect my mom to ruin all my long jeans and nice pants but I was reduced to two different outfits—a light-colored pair of jeans that had somewhat worn knees. Mom did not have a problem cutting up my old play jeans. However, she was not about to mutilate a pair of Old Navy jeans. So, the thrift shop and Target became our department stores of choice. I admired my mother's thriftiness with money but I was very concerned about how I was going to look everyday for six weeks. But my mom performed miracles on the new and almost-new pants she got me. With a pair of scissors and safety pins she managed to adjust the right leg to my now fat sock. I did manage to try to wear a different tee-shirt every day in order to not call too much attention to my legs. I usually picked long and baggy shirts hoping that when I got up to use my crutches, they would cover me to my knees—but that was impossible. I also knew that wearing a disguise would not work, so my sunglasses did not help at all. At the time I wished that Halloween was celebrated for a whole month. That way I could have worn all sorts of fantastic outfits to school. Instead I got used to seeing myself in the same two pairs of pants five days a week for over six weeks.

Nighttime was a relief. I could wear the baggiest pajama bottoms and slip them over my leg easily. My Teta (Grandmother in Arabic) brought me a couple of bright colored pairs with astronauts and dinosaurs—my favorites. The bottoms had string around the waist so I lived in those during the weekends.

Sunday was another day of humiliation because I looked pretty grungy going to church in my new togs. Again, my family was sensitive to my needs and we switched to an earlier service to avoid the congestion and allow me to deal with the crutches better. Again, my clothes selection was extremely narrow.

There was one bright spot in my wardrobe. I

was given a pair of bright yellow trunks which had an elastic waistband and an elastic brief under the wide legs that came to my knees. These slipped over my big sock fairly easy and I wore them when I wanted to look a bit cheerful. Unfortunately they got pretty worn out after a few times at the playground during the weekends and the holes on my bottom were not pretty. At least that is what Nicole said because I could not see myself from behind!

Sometimes my mind would wander, thinking about kids who are permanently in a wheelchair and have to wear basic clothing in order to cope with twisted bodies or small limbs. When I thought about these kids, I felt ashamed for complaining about my situation. Gradually I like to think I matured a little and I began to focus on my school work again since I could not do any soccer, skate boarding, bicycling or other physical activities. I even got back to my piano lessons once I learned how to use the foot pedal with my left foot because my right one would hit the pedal and virtually get stuck on it until I leaned over and picked it up and put it on the side. Eventually my life became, if not normal, routine again.

Episode 5: Time's Up

At the end of four weeks, I went for a thorough checkup. I had hopes that my physical weight would be reduced. I got wheeled in for x-rays and when they were ready, the doctor and my dad were busy discussing the progress on my broken ankle while I became interested in studying the picture on the lighted wall fixture which showed my leg. I kept trying to get the doctor's attention and my dad's to point out that I had a rock lodged on the side of my foot near my ankle—something I had complained about but was dismissed by my parents. It was hard to get a word in while they were talking. Finally I tugged at my dad and said, "Look, there's the rock that's been causing my itching and aching." I had actually experimented with a coat hanger trying to relieve my misery only to have my parents say, "It's nothing, try to ignore it. It will get better." Suddenly there was a pause in the adult conversation and both heads rotated toward the exposed picture of my leg. I could hear a chuckle from the doctor and my dad just said, "Wow, he's had that there for a while."

Once they agreed the little rock, much smaller than the first knuckle of my little finger, was there, the doctor suggested that I could go into a smaller cast. I almost cried out loud until my dad quickly said, "Great, he'll be able to move a lot easier with less weight." The doctor agreed and my Big Sock was cut open with a small electric saw. But when my whole leg was exposed, it looked smaller than the left leg and I gasped at the sight. The doctor gave me a big smile and said, "There is no problem here. Remember that your leg has been confined in that big cast for a long time. In a couple of weeks, you won't be able to see the difference." I had no choice but to believe him.

The new sock was more of a knee sock. It only came up to my knee and it did not seem as thick as the old one. My toes were still exposed but by now they were quite used to it! My dad tried to make conversation on the way back home but I was just too disappointed that I had not healed quicker and was out of a cast altogether. When we got home, both Mom and Nicole were full of wonderful thoughts about how easy it was for me to get around now even without crutches. So I guess that was a positive way to look at things. Also, they pointed out that I could probably wear some of my regular shorts without having to tear them open. A lot of my disappointment faded a little.

Yes, I went through a whole new signing of autographs in school so that gave me some much-needed attention because by now everyone had gotten used to my hobbling along at a turtle's pace and I was gingerly ignored.

The next two weeks did not drag too much. I was busy with a piano recital and that proved to be fun, because when I came onto the stage the audience gave a little gasp of sympathy for me because I was in a cast. I had to pause until they adjusted to seeing me in my new cast, and then I settled down to entertain them with my piano playing. That went well and afterwards I got even more attention and congratulations from everyone in attendance. Isn't it terrible how we need attention? But it is also good because it makes you feel very nice inside.

About a day or two before I was to go for my final leg undressing, we were invited to some friends who have a pool, and I must admit that I did something rather foolish. Yes, I jumped in the pool before I realized that I was sinking, sinking, sinking due to the weight on my right leg. I pushed myself upward and yelled out to my folks who came to the rescue but not with big smiles. The cast was a mess; it was dripping and decomposing at the same time. Well, a quick towel wrap and a very quiet drive to the hospital found me at the emergency room again. This time my folks were not too happy with me. They thought I had done this on purpose to get the cast off sooner.

Well, as it turned out, not too much harm was done according to the nurses and doctor who saw me. They proceeded to take the remains of the withered cast off. Then I was told to get up and stand on my foot. My leg and foot felt so weird without the weight that my knee literally crumbled under me. I lost my balance and the doctor caught me just in time. I started to cry because I thought now I'd really done it. I would have to have another cast. Not so according to the doctor. He said that with physical therapy and patience, I would be as normal as any kid in my classroom. All I could think of was, "I don't believe him!"

I was released from the hospital. And what I had thought would be my happiest day after six weeks of misery with all that weight off, proved to be a day of doom and gloom. I felt cheated. I felt people had lied to me. Sure, I didn't have the weight to worry about, and I could pick anything in my closet to wear, but I could not put any weight on my right leg. I began to think it was a permanent condition.

That first night did have some highlights—I could bathe all by myself without a plastic cover over my right leg and I was able to soak in the tub with warm water and relax for what seemed a long time. I guess the warm water worked wonders because when I went to get out of the tub I realized that my right leg had more feeling, and although it still looked skinner than my left leg, I was able to hoist myself up and put a little pressure on it. What followed after my bath was a wonderful treat that my parents had planned. They gave me a great massage on my legs and that, too, worked miracles. Slowly, I began to gain confidence in what the doctor had said.

The next couple of weeks I still relied on my crutches a bit but with the physical therapy and all the help at home, I was beginning to feel normal. And, I must say, it was not long before I was treated normally at home as well. I was expected to assume some of my chores and the leg excuse did not go over very well after eight weeks of catering to me. So by the tenth week after my accident I joined my "normal" world once again. I wasn't ready to make goals in soccer but I did manage to get out and move around with the rest of my team. Nobody made fun of me for being slow and clumsy and that was good.

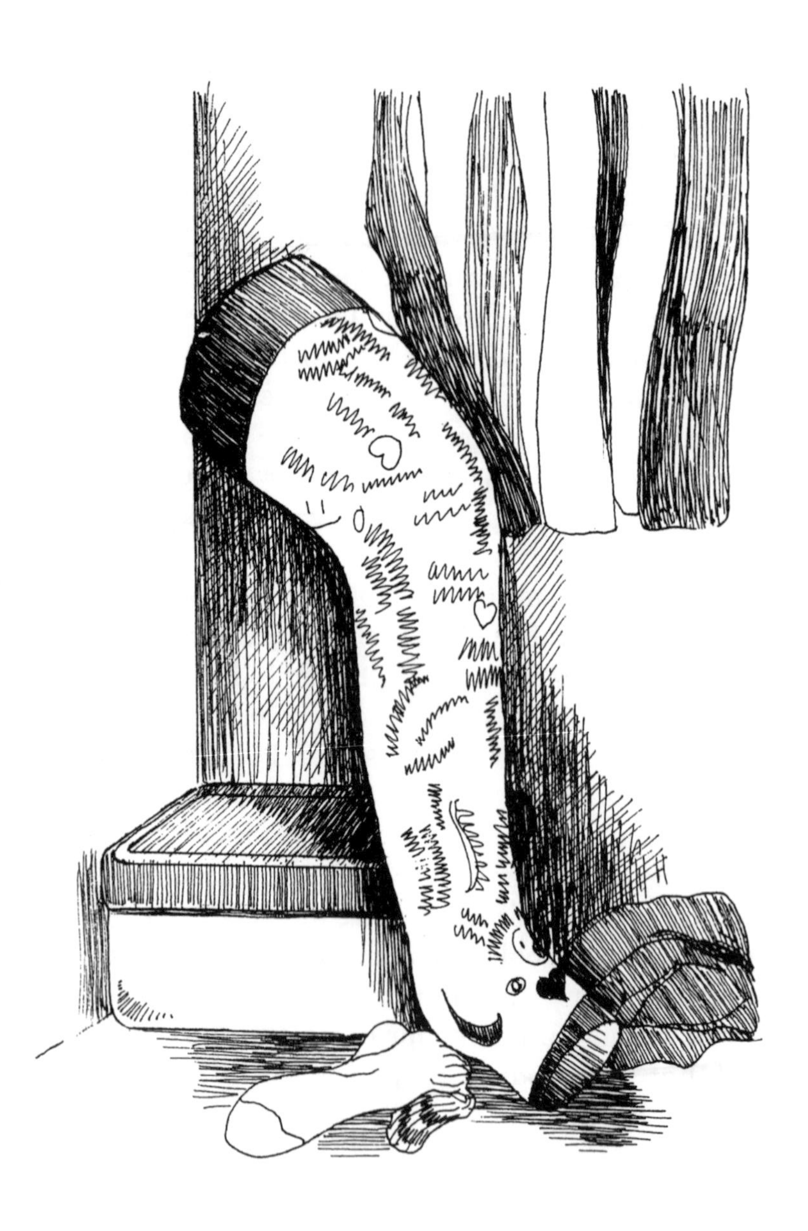

The final x-ray showed no sign of a break on my ankle and now, six months later, I have resumed all my activities. I still worry about the kids who are less fortunate than I am. My Big Sock sits in the corner of my closet as a friendly reminder of my weeks of carrying all that extra weight. I sure don't wish my kind of accident on anyone. I am grateful that my family sure helped me through it. I was a real pill at times when I look back! But I'd never admit it to them!!

THE END

P.S. A special thanks to my grandson Alexander for sharing this mishap with me.